For Amel, Aya, and Ali. I love you.
Love, Daddy

Balzer + Bray is an imprint of HarperCollins Publishers.

Baby Bear
Copyright © 2014 by Kadir Nelson
All rights reserved. Manufactured in China.
No part of this book may be used or reproduced in any manner whatsoever without written permission except in the case of
brief quotations embodied in critical articles and reviews. For information address HarperCollins Children's Books, a division of
HarperCollins Publishers, 10 East 53rd Street, New York, NY 10022.
www.harpercollinschildrens.com

Library of Congress Cataloging-in-Publication Data
Nelson, Kadir, author, illustrator.
    Baby Bear / words and paintings by Kadir Nelson. — First edition.
        pages   cm
    Summary: As Baby Bear tries to find his way home through the forest, he asks many different woodland creatures for help and
finds that much of their advice is more comforting than helpful.
    ISBN 978-0-06-224172-6 (hardcover bdg.)
    [1. Lost children—Fiction.   2. Bears—Fiction.   3. Forest animals—Fiction.]   I. Title.
PZ7.N43446Bab   2014   2013003083
[E]—dc23   CIP
                                                                                                                          AC

The artist used oil on canvas to create the illustrations for this book.
Typography by Martha Rago. Hand lettering by Iskra Johnson
13 14 15 16 17   SCP   10 9 8 7 6 5 4 3 2 1
❖
First Edition

Baby Bear

Kadir Nelson

Balzer + Bray
an imprint of HarperCollinsPublishers

Excuse me, dear Mountain Lion. I'm lost.
Can you help me find my way home?

Oh, is that so? Well, Baby Bear, when I am lost
I try to retrace my steps. Can you remember
how you got here?

Hmm, I wasn't paying attention. But I think it is that way.

Then perhaps you should go that way.

Thank you, dear Lion.

You're welcome, Baby Bear.

Excuse me, dear Frog. I am lost.
Can you help me find my way home?

Do you mind? I am busy.

But I'm lost and afraid.

Do not be afraid, Baby Bear. Trust yourself. You will find
your way home. Now please, if you don't mind . . .

Thank you, sir.

Excuse me, dear Squirrels.
Can you help me? I'm lost.
It is very hard to choose
which way to go.

When I am lost I hug a tree
and think of home.

But isn't every tree your home?

Why, yes.

But which way shall I go?

That is a good question.
Choose wisely.

Hug a tree? Ha, ha!
That's just silly!

Hello, Baby Bear.
What are you doing?

Uh, nothing.

Are you lost?

Yes, I think so.

When I am lost, I sit very still and try
to listen to my heart. It speaks as softly
and as sweetly as a gentle breeze. And
it is never wrong. It will lead you home.

Thank you, dear Moose.

You're welcome, Baby Bear.

Hello, Baby Bear. Why are you crying?

I'm lost, and I can't find my way home.

*Oh, I see. When I am lost, I climb a little higher so
I can see all around. Keep walking, Baby Bear.
You are closer than you think. And sing a song—
it will make you feel better.*

Thank you, dear Ram.

My word. Who was that singing so beautifully?

It was me. I am lost and alone.

You are not alone, Baby Bear. I am here with you.
You only need look up and keep going. You will
find your way home.

Thank you, dear Owl. I love you.

I love you too, Baby Bear.

Hello, Baby Bear.

Oh! Hello, dear Salmon. I'm trying to
find my way home. Can you help me?

Yes, you are very close.

I am?

*Yes, you are. If you promise not to
eat me, I will show you the way.*

I promise.

Follow me.

Climb up there, Baby Bear.

Can you see?

Yes, I can see.
I AM home.